P9-CLR-432

Care Bears™

STORYBOOK TREASURY

Care Bears™

STORYBOOK TREASURY

SCHOLASTIC INC.
New York Toronto London Auckland Sydney
Mexico City New Delhi Hong Kong Buenos Aires

ISBN 0-439-62486-X

Designed by Joan Moloney

12 11 10 9 8 7 6 5 4 4 5 6 7 8/0

Printed in the U.S.A.
First printing, February 2004

Contents

Care Bears™

STORYBOOK TREASURY

by Nancy Parent
Illustrated by David Stein

One day, Cheer Bear decided to hold a Care-a-lot caring contest. "A prize will go to the bear who shows the best way to care," she said.

The Care Bears took the contest very seriously. Friend Bear was the first to see a way to care. "I think caring means taking turns with a favorite toy," she said.

Share Bear cared by making sure she had enough treats for everyone. "Help yourself!" she said as she passed out yummy rainbow bars.

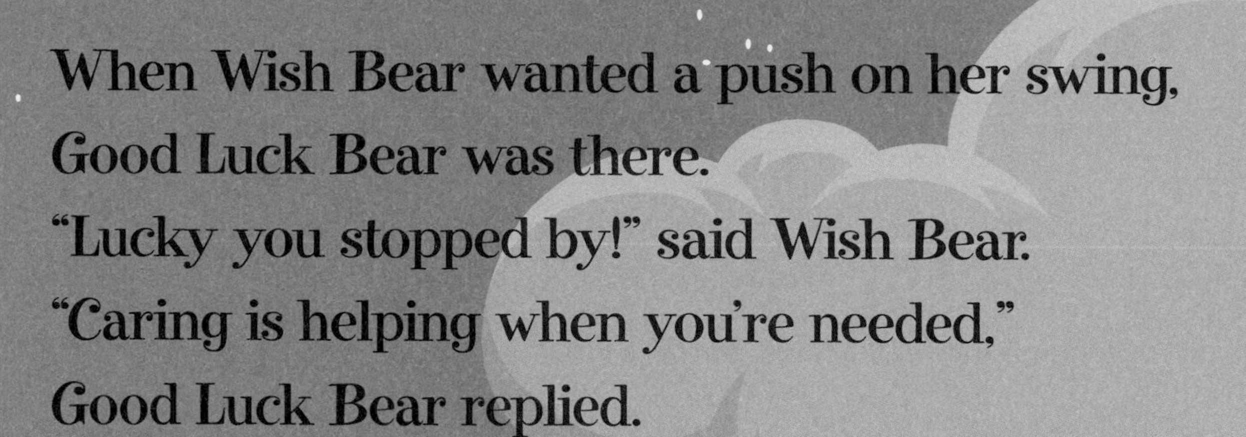

When Wish Bear wanted a push on her swing,
Good Luck Bear was there.
"Lucky you stopped by!" said Wish Bear.
"Caring is helping when you're needed,"
Good Luck Bear replied.

During an afternoon storm, Grumpy Bear saw a way to care for Friend Bear. "Caring," said Grumpy Bear, "is sharing your umbrella in the rain."

When Share Bear didn't feel well, some of her friends visited her. "Comforting someone who is sick shows you really care," Tenderheart Bear said.

"Caring is making someone laugh when he's sad," said Funshine Bear. He juggled stars to cheer up Grumpy Bear.

"I can show I care by letting you go ahead of me in line," Wish Bear told Love-a-lot Bear. "I'd love to!" said Love-a-lot Bear. "Thanks!"

When Wish Bear couldn't fall asleep at naptime, Bedtime Bear read her a sweet dreams story to show he cared.

SWEET DREAMS
SWEET DREAMS

Love-a-lot Bear showed how to care by giving Tenderheart Bear a great big hug. “I love you, Tenderheart Bear,” she said.

Cheer Bear thought all the Care Bears had done a wonderful job of caring. But who should she pick as the winner of the contest?

First Annual
Care-a-lot
Caring Contest

Cheer Bear made her announcement: "The winners of the Care-a-lot caring contest are . . . all of you! Because everyone wins when everyone cares for others!" Then she proudly handed out the prizes.

"Now we can show how much we care by sharing these prizes with our friends!" all the Care Bears said together. And that's just what they did.

Three cheers for caring, Care Bears!

Care Bears™

What Makes You Happy?

by J. E. Bright

Close your eyes
and think of
something
that makes
you happy.

Do you love playing outside on a beautiful day? That's something that makes Funshine Bear very happy!

Do you love relaxing and daydreaming, like Wish Bear?

XOXO

Does it make you happy to help a friend with a project? Grumpy Bear enjoys helping Share Bear by holding her ladder.

Do you love flying a kite on a perfect summer afternoon? Nothing makes Love-a-lot Bear happier!

Cheer Bear loves to juggle stars and make her friends smile. Do you love to cheer up your friends, too?

Do you love to paint a beautiful picture, like Friend Bear?

Tenderheart Bear's favorite thing is spreading love all over Care-a-lot. Does telling people you love them make you happy, too?

Is it playing with your friends that makes you happiest? Share Bear loves to rollerskate with Cheer Bear and Grumpy Bear.

Does it make you happy to hope for something good to happen? Good Luck Bear likes to do that—and sometimes what he hopes for comes true!

Bedtime Bear is happiest when he's snug in bed and having a sweet dream. Do you love that, too?

Happiness is best when it is shared, so tell somebody special what makes you happy. You'll be glad you did!

Care Bears™

Find That Rainbow!

by Sonia Sander
Illustrated by Duendes del Sur

Cheer Bear's favorite rainbow has disappeared.

"I think I see your rainbow," said Wish Bear.

But it was only Bedtime Bear singing the birds to sleep.

"Look!" said Bedtime Bear. "There's your rainbow."

"No, that's Love-a-lot Bear painting," said Cheer Bear.

Love-a-lot Bear thought she saw Cheer Bear's rainbow.
But it was only Friend Bear carrying a bouquet of flowers.

"I've spotted your rainbow!" cried Friend Bear.

"No," said Cheer Bear. "Those are Good Luck Bear's butterflies."

"Over there is the rainbow," said Good Luck Bear. But Good Luck Bear had mistaken Funshine Bear's balloons for the rainbow.

"There it is!" said Funshine Bear. "There's your rainbow!"

"That's not a rainbow, either." Cheer Bear sighed. "That's Share Bear bringing lollipops for everyone."

Share Bear thought she saw Cheer Bear's rainbow just above the clouds.
But it turned out to be Tenderheart Bear's roller skates.

"Look up in the sky," said Tenderheart Bear. "There is your rainbow."

"No. Those are raindrops," Cheer Bear said sadly.

"I just knew it was going to rain today," said Grumpy Bear. "That's why I brought my umbrella."

Cheer Bear smiled. "I just remembered what shows up after a rain shower."

A RAINBOW!

by Frances Ann Ladd
Illustrated by Jay Johnson

A big fat raindrop landed on Grumpy Bear's nose with a plop.

"The rain's going to spoil everything," he sighed. "What an unlucky day for a picnic."

"Don't worry, Grumpy Bear," said Good Luck Bear.
"Every cloud has a silver lining."
"What do you mean?" asked Grumpy Bear.

"I mean something good will come of the rain," said Good Luck Bear. "Just you wait!"

“And there it is!” said Cheer Bear.

"A beautiful rainbow to ride down to our picnic!"

"Whee!"

Laughing, the Care Bears landed in a heap at Share Bear's feet.

"What's the matter?" asked Cheer Bear.
"I brought five sunshine bars and five rainbow bars, and they all broke in two," said Share Bear.

"What terrible luck," said Grumpy Bear.
"Remember, every cloud has a silver lining,"
said Good Luck Bear.

“Yum!” shouted Funshine Bear. “Now we can each taste both treats!”

"Come with us to the picnic, Bedtime Bear!"
said Share Bear.

“I can’t. I lost my starry nightcap, and I have to find it,” said Bedtime Bear.

"Oh, dear, more bad luck," said Grumpy Bear.

"Good luck won't be far behind," said Good Luck Bear, smiling. "We just have to look for it."

"And for Bedtime Bear's missing cap!" said Friend Bear.

“Look, I found our missing picnic blanket!” said Share Bear. “That’s lucky for us,” said Cheer Bear. “We never would have found the blanket if Bedtime Bear hadn’t lost his nightcap.”

“But we still haven’t found my cap,” said Bedtime Bear.

"There it is!" shouted Good Luck Bear.
"And what a perfect spot for a picnic!"
said Cheer Bear.

"Double the good luck!" said Funshine Bear.

"Now the only bad luck is that Tenderheart Bear, Wish Bear, and Love-a-lot Bear aren't here yet," said Good Luck Bear.

“What’s the silver lining in that?” wondered Grumpy Bear.

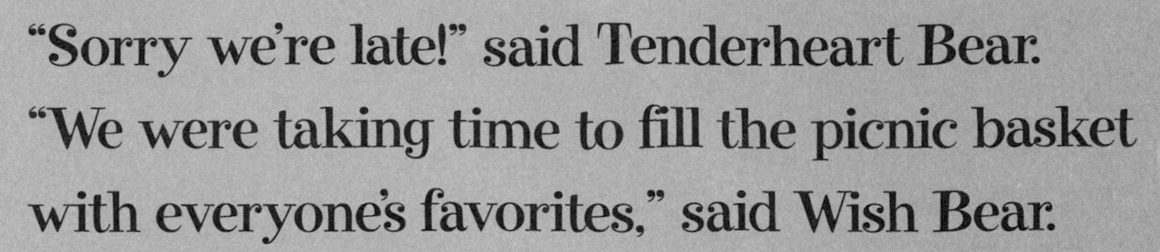

"Sorry we're late!" said Tenderheart Bear. "We were taking time to fill the picnic basket with everyone's favorites," said Wish Bear.

"And making enough rainbow punch for everyone," said Love-a-lot Bear.

"Every cloud really does have a silver lining!" said Grumpy Bear.

"And this one is delicious!" said Good Luck Bear.

by Sonia Sander
Illustrated by David Stein

It's the start of a busy, busy, sunny day in Care-a-lot. "Rise and shine!" calls out Love-a-lot Bear.

Cheer Bear can't wait to say
good morning to all of her friends.
"Hip, hip, hooray! It's a beautiful day!"

The sun smiles down on the Care Bears,
showering them with sunlit kisses.
Cheer Bear hurries to collect hearts.
"Catch them all!" roots Good Luck Bear.

Tenderheart Bear invites everyone to join his roller-skating train. "I hope Tenderheart Bear is watching where he's going," worries Grumpy Bear. "Just remember to hold on tight with all your might!" Share Bear tells him.

Zipping, zooming, round and round they go.

"Special delivery!" says Share Bear.
"Yum!" shouts Tenderheart Bear.
"Snack time is my favorite!"

All is quiet in Care-a-lot
while the Care Bears happily
eat their cupcakes.

“Hop on, Wish Bear,” says
Good Luck Bear.
“I’ll swing you through the
twinkling stars.”
“Whee!” Wish Bear laughs.

"Do you want to go next, Love-a-lot Bear?"
asks Wish Bear.
"Everyone can have a turn reaching for
the stars," says Funshine Bear.

Soon the sun goes down.
It's time for best friends to say good night.
"I can't wait until tomorrow," says Friend Bear.
"Then we can play all day all over again."

As Wish Bear sends
the first shooting
stars across the sky
she makes a wish,
for another bright
and sunny day.

Bedtime Bear dusts the sky with sweet dreams for all the Care Bears in Care-a-lot.

"Good night. Sleep tight," says Bedtime Bear. "The sun will be up and shining again before we know it."

Care Bears™

The Day Nobody Shared

by Nancy Parent

Illustrated by Jay Johnson

One day, Good Luck Bear got a box of rainbow bars in the mail.

He decided to hide the treats so he could have them all to himself.

"Hello," said Share Bear. "What are you doing?"

"I'm hiding my rainbow bars so I don't have to share them," Good Luck Bear whispered.

"But it feels so good to share," said Share Bear.

"It does?" asked Good Luck Bear.

"Come for a ride on the swings," said Share Bear.
"I'll tell you a story called The Day Nobody Shared."

Once upon a time, Cheer Bear made a giant ice-cream sundae with rainbow sprinkles that she wouldn't share with any of her friends.

Cheer Bear ended up with an awful tummy ache from eating the ice cream all by herself.

Then Bedtime Bear refused to share his special spot to watch the Care-a-lot parade.

But without Grumpy Bear to keep him awake, Bedtime Bear fell asleep and missed the whole thing!

That afternoon, Tenderheart Bear wouldn't share his toys, so nobody wanted to play with him.

Tenderheart Bear quickly got bored. "Toys don't laugh and talk like friends," he said unhappily.

And when Love-a-lot Bear wouldn't share her kite with Funshine Bear, he went and played with Wish Bear instead.

"What bad luck that no one wanted to share," said Good Luck Bear.

"That's right," said Share Bear.

"If I share my rainbow bars," Good Luck Bear asked, "will that make everyone happy?"

"Yes," said Share Bear. "Sharing takes happiness and spreads it around. Sweetness goes a long way, if you're willing to share."

"I want to share these rainbow bars with our friends right now!" said Good Luck Bear.

"Great idea!" Share Bear replied. "We can throw a sharing party in the park!"

When they passed Share Bear's house, Share Bear ran inside and came out with a bunch of balloons. "I'm going to share these!" said Share Bear.

"It feels really great to share," said Good Luck Bear.

"And it tastes yummy, too!" said Share Bear.

Care Bears™

Who's Who?

Love-a-lot Bear

Funshine Bear

Wish Bear

by Sonia Sander
Illustrated by Duendes del Sur

Which unselfish Care Bear is
always willing to share?
Share Bear!

Whose sunny smile shines bright
day in and day out?
Funshine Bear!

Whose red heart proves he cares
for each and every Care Bear?
Tenderheart Bear!

Which Care Bear's good-luck charm is his four-leaf clover?

Good Luck Bear!

Who has two pink hearts to show
how much she loves every Care Bear?
Love-a-lot Bear!

Who is every Care Bear's
best friend?
Friend Bear!

Which grumpy Care Bear
has his very own rain cloud?
Grumpy Bear!

Which Care Bear's shooting star
can make wishes come true?
Wish Bear!

Who brings good cheer
to all of the Care Bears?
Cheer Bear!

Whose good-night stories bring
sweet dreams to sleepy bears?
Bedtime Bear!

Care Bears™

Special Delivery

by Quinlan B. Lee
Illustrated by Jay Johnson

"Hooray!" said Love-a-lot Bear. "This is my favorite day of the year."

"Mine too," said Tenderheart Bear. "I love spending the day telling all of our friends how much we love them."

"Do you have all our special hearts ready to be delivered?" asked Love-a-lot Bear.

"I sure do," Tenderheart Bear replied. "The first one is for Funshine Bear. He shouldn't be too hard to find."

"Have you seen Funshine Bear?" they asked Wish Bear. "I wish I had," she answered. "Keep looking and I know you'll find him."

"Thanks," said Love-a-lot Bear. "I love how you always give such good wishes." She gave Wish Bear her special heart.

Tenderheart Bear and Love-a-lot Bear looked in the Cloud Patch. But they only found Bedtime Bear.

"I love that Bedtime Bear naps during the day so that he can help us all to sleep the whole night through," whispered Love-a-lot Bear.

“Have you seen Funshine Bear?” Tenderheart Bear asked. “No, but I will keep an eye out for him,” Friend Bear replied.

"You're such a good friend. You're always willing to lend a helping hand," said Tenderheart Bear as he gave Friend Bear her heart.

"This is fun, but I'm getting hungry," Love-a-lot Bear said.
"Would you like some of my rainbow bars?" Share Bear asked.

"Thank you, Share Bear," said Tenderheart Bear. "That's what I love about you best. You are always willing to share."

Tenderheart Bear and Love-a-lot Bear slid down one rainbow slide after another looking for Funshine Bear.

"We're never going to find him," sighed Tenderheart Bear.

"Finding a friend can be hard sometimes," Grumpy Bear said.
"But keep looking!" said Cheer Bear. "I just know that you'll find Funshine Bear soon."

"You two are such good friends to turn our grumpies into grins," Tenderheart Bear said, smiling. He gave them each a special heart.

"You're in luck!" said Good Luck Bear, "I just saw Funshine Bear peeking out from behind that cloud over there."

"Thank you," said Tenderheart Bear.
"We love that you always help things turn out right," said Love-a-lot Bear.

Love-a-lot Bear and Tenderheart Bear laughed and laughed when Funshine Bear jumped out from behind the cloud and surprised them.

"Funshine Bear, you made today extra fun," said Love-a-lot Bear. "We love that about you."

"We did it," said Tenderheart Bear. "We delivered hearts to all our friends."

"Not everyone," said Funshine Bear.
"Who did we miss?" asked Love-a-lot Bear.

"You!" cried all the Care Bears together. "You remind us how important it is to tell everyone how much you love them. And that's what we love best about you."